THE CHILDREN'S CLASSICS Collection

Dados Internacionais de Catalogação na Publicação (CIP) de acordo com ISBD

S516b Sewell, Anna.
Black Beauty / Anna Sewell. - Jandira, SP : W. Books, 2025.
120 p. ; 12,80cm x 19,80cm. - (Classics).

ISBN: 978-65-5294-120-6

1. Literatura inglesa. 2. Aventura. 3. Clássicos. 4. Histórias. 5. Emoções. I. Título. II. Série.

2025-2480 CDD 823.91
CDU 821.111-3

Elaborada por Lucio Feitosa - CRB-8/8803
Índice para catálogo sistemático:
1. Literatura inglesa 823.91
2. Literatura inglesa 821.111-3

Text based on the original story by Anna Sewell,
adapted by Gemma Barder
Illustrations by Archina Laezza

1st edition in 2025
www.cirandacultural.com.br

BLACK BEAUTY

Anna Sewell

W. Books

Black Beauty

A handsome black horse

Duchess

Black Beauty's mother

Ginger

A chestnut horse

Merrylegs

An old grey pony

Captain

An experienced taxi horse

Farmer Grey

Owner of the farm where Black Beauty was born

The Gordons

A wealthy family

John

A groom

Joe

A stableboy

Jerry

A taxi driver

The Earl and Duchess of Westland

A wealthy family

Skinner

A horse for hire man

Mr Thoroughgood

A farmer

Miss Ellen and Miss Blomefield

Kind women

Chapter One

My first memory is of the meadow. A lush green field with a clear pond in the middle and large trees which gave plenty of shade for when Mother and I got hot.

My mother was called Duchess. We lived together at Farmer Grey's farm and each day she would teach me everything I needed to become a good horse. 'Stay calm, stand tall, don't kick

and *never* bite your master,' she told me.

As soon as I was old enough to eat grass, Mother was sent back to work pulling Farmer Grey's carriage. I was put into a field with some other young horses who liked to jump about and run wild.

Each night, Mother and I would settle together in our stable, and she would tell me not to act like the carthorses I was playing with all day. I was a special horse, she said, and I had to act with more dignity.

When I turned four, a rich man from a neighbouring house came to see me. He nodded and smiled as he looked me over and I stood still and proud just as my mother had taught me. I learned that the man's name was Squire Gordon.

'He's a fine horse, Mr Grey,' said Squire Gordon. 'As black as night, apart from the white diamond shape on his nose and one white foot. Quite extraordinary. He'll look very fine pulling my carriage – once he is broken in, of course.'

Although I did not like the sound of being "broken in", I felt proud at Mr Gordon's words. I did not know then, of course, that if Squire Gordon really did want me to pull his carriage, it would mean leaving Farmer Grey's, and my mother, forever.

'Do not fret,' said Mother as we lay in the stables that night. I was now big enough to have my own stall, but we were still side by side as always. 'Squire Gordon is a good man. He will look after you, as long as you are well-behaved and good to him too.'

The following day, my training

began. First, Farmer Grey placed a bridle over my head. I did not like it much at first, but I had seen Mother wear one many times, so I let him do what was needed. It felt odd, but I soon got used to it. Next, I had my very first pair of shoes fitted. Although it did not hurt when the blacksmith hammered the iron horseshoes onto my hooves, they felt heavy when I moved. Finally, Farmer Grey gently strapped a saddle to my back and taught me how it was to be ridden.

A few weeks later, Farmer Grey harnessed me to his carriage next to Mother. Together we trotted through the lanes, keeping in step with each other perfectly.

'You have done well, my son,' said Mother. 'But Farmer Grey is a skilled rider, and he knows horses well. Not everyone you meet will be the same, but if you keep your temper and stay strong, you will be all right, no matter what comes your way.'

Chapter Two

Finally, the day came when Squire Gordon was to take me away. I could not imagine a life without Mother, and although I was excited to see what would come next, I whinnied as I left our stable for the last time. The only thing I could do was to keep Mother's voice in my head and do my best to make her proud.

Birtwick was a large, grey stone house with a circular gravel driveway. It was far grander than Farmer Grey's farm and I raised my head a little higher as I trotted down to the stables. Squire Gordon handed me over to the groom. 'There you are, John, didn't I tell you he was a handsome horse?'

John was a young man with a kind face and strong arms. He gave me a good groom, and gently placed a saddle on my back. We rode around

groom

A person whose job is to take care of horses or a stable.

the rolling fields that surrounded Birtwick and I could tell John was testing me. He watched how I behaved when we jumped over fences and rivers, and how I responded to each gentle kick and pull on the reins.

‘Well, sir, you can tell he’s been well brought up,’ said John, as Squire Gordon met us in the stable yard after our ride. ‘He has a gentle temper, but he’s strong, too. He’ll do just fine with Ginger on the carriage, and I think Mrs Gordon might like to ride him.’

Squire Gordon raised his eyebrows in pleased surprise. ‘Well then, you had better go and introduce him to the rest of the horses,’ he said.

I was to share my stables with two other horses. Merrylegs was in the stall next to mine. He was a short, grey pony who had been at Birtwick for many years. It was his job to pull the pony trap and to be ridden by Squire and Mrs Gordon's two young daughters. He was a happy horse and made

me feel welcome as I looked around my new home.

Ginger, however, was not so welcoming. She was a tall, chestnut horse with a sleek mane and sharp eyes. 'That was my stall,' she said, snorting. 'You have kicked me out!'

'I'm sorry,' I replied. 'I did not know.' I did not want to make an enemy on my first day, but Ginger turned her head away.

Merrylegs assured me that John was going to move Ginger to a different stall whether I had arrived or not. Ginger had

a habit of biting, and the young ladies of the house were refusing to come into the stables while she was in the stall by the door. I wondered how such a beautiful horse could do something as rude as biting. 'She was badly treated before she came to Birtwick,' Merrylegs explained in a low voice. 'Her master did not train her well, but John has done a good job taming her, as much as he can.'

The next morning, John led Ginger and me into the stable yard to where Squire and Mrs Gordon were waiting for us. Mrs Gordon stroked the white diamond on my nose, and I gently nuzzled her hand. 'He's beautiful, John!'

Mrs Gordon said, delighted. 'I believe that is what we should call him. Black Beauty.'

Chapter Three

Ginger and I were harnessed onto the Gordons' fine carriage. It was heavier than Farmer Grey's one, but I soon got used to the new weight and pace. At first, Ginger's ears flattened irritably when we stood side by side, but as we trotted in time and she saw that I could pull as well as she could, she started to soften.

'I hear Farmer Grey is a good master,' Ginger said at last.

'He is,' I replied.

'I am sorry if I was not very welcoming to you,' said Ginger. 'When I meet someone new, I don't know if they are going to be kind or hurtful.'

I stayed silent as the carriage pulled up in front of another large house. Mr and Mrs Gordon got out of the carriage and went inside. John led us to a water trough at the side of the house. 'I don't like to bite,' said Ginger. 'Sometimes I can't help it. Do you ever bite?'

trough

A long, narrow open container used for serving food or water to animals.

'No,' I replied. 'Mother taught me not to.'

Ginger looked sad for a moment. 'Perhaps if I had not been taken from my mother as soon as I was born, I might have learned from her, too.'

From that day on, Ginger and I became friends. As soon as she saw I was there to work hard for the Gordons and not cause her any trouble, she began to relax. We spent our days happily together, and our evenings with Merrylegs in the stables, swapping stories and keeping each other company.

Mrs Gordon began taking me out when she went riding, while Mr Gordon rode Ginger. We had

many happy trips together across the Gordons' estate and sometimes we would ride to the top field where I could see Farmer Grey's land and catch a glimpse of Mother in our meadow.

As autumn drew in, the weather changed. One wet and windy day, John was ordered to harness me to the dog cart. It was smaller than the carriage, so only took one horse to drive it. Squire Gordon was going away on a business trip for a night, and I was to take him to town.

We rode further than I had ever done before. The rain had made the roads slick with mud, and soon we came to a bridge that was almost submerged under the rising river water.

'Take it easy, sir!' said the bridge attendant, slowly beckoning us onto the wooden bridge. I was frightened but I could see the bridge was still strong, so I stepped slowly across.

The rest of the journey passed by without any difficulty and soon we had reached town. Squire Gordon was staying at a hotel, and the hotel grooms took special care of me, making sure my coat was dry and I was fed, before they settled me down for the night.

I was well rested, which was a good thing because the journey home the following day was worse than the day before. It had not stopped raining all night and it took us twice as long to reach the river. The water had risen so high that I could not see if the bridge was still safe to cross.

I backed away slightly from the river. Not too much in case I scared my master, but enough to tell him that I did not think the bridge was safe.

'Come now, Beauty!' said Squire Gordon. 'It's just a little water, nothing to fear!' He guided me to the bridge once more. I took one step onto the wooden planks and backed away again, more forcefully this time. All my senses told me that the bridge was not safe. I refused to cross it.

‘Beauty! What are you doing?’ Squire Gordon said, and it pained me to hear the frustration in his voice. At that moment, the bridge attendant appeared at the other side of the river. He was waving his arms above his head and shouting through the rain.

'Do not cross, sir!' he yelled. 'Do *not* cross!'

'Why ever not, man?' Squire Gordon yelled back.

'The bridge has collapsed in the middle!' came the reply.

Squire Gordon was silent for a moment. Then he looked down at me in wonder. 'Good boy, Beauty!'

he said, patting my neck as we turned away from the bridge. 'I don't know how you knew it, but you have saved my life for sure and certain.'

It took us a long time to return to Birtwick. Two more bridges had been lost to the rising river waters, and when we finally found a place to cross it was almost nightfall.

When we arrived home, Mrs Gordon ran out of the house with a lamp, her face panic-stricken. 'We have been so worried!' she cried as Squire Gordon dismounted. 'Where have you been?'

Squire Gordon told his wife the whole story, and when John came to take me to the stables, he instructed him to give me a good groom and some warm bran mash (a mixture of oats, warm water and other treats like carrots), which I loved.

Although I was cold, wet and exhausted, I felt proud, too. When I returned to the stables, Ginger whinnied and moved about in her stall. 'There now, Ginger,' said John. 'He's back now with no harm done, no need to worry.'

When I was settled in for the night, Ginger snorted. 'I wasn't worried,' she said haughtily.

'Yes, you were!' teased Merrylegs. 'I might be an old pony, but I can still read you like a book, missy.'

I knew by now not to make Ginger any more annoyed than she already was. It was enough for me to know that she was worried about me, so I stayed silent and fell asleep. Safe, warm and with a full stomach.

Chapter Four

My days at Birtwick with Ginger and Merrylegs passed happily. Christmas came and went with trips and parties to attend. Soon, spring came and with it, a new stable boy to help John with his duties.

'Joe Green?' asked John when Squire Gordon told him who would be helping from now on. 'But he's only fourteen. He knows nothing about horses.'

Squire Gordon smiled. 'And neither did you when you first came to us,' he replied. 'You learnt from a groom, just as Joe will learn from you.'

John nodded, remembering that good grooms are made by good teachers.

'Joe's family need him to bring in some money, and he's a decent lad. Teach him what you know.'

Joe joined the stables a few days later. He was small, but willing.

He had bright red hair and his faced flushed when John gave him the harder jobs to do, like clearing out our stalls and putting in fresh hay. After a few weeks, it was clear that Joe was a hard worker, so when Squire Gordon was once again called away on business, John was happy for Joe to stay behind to look after Merrylegs and me, while Ginger pulled the dog cart. On Mrs Gordon's instructions, John had to drive the cart this time, in case anything bad happened on the journey.

Life was peaceful at Birtwick, especially when Squire Gordon was away. Mrs Gordon and her daughters sometimes went to visit friends, but generally it was a time when the horses who stayed behind could rest. Squire Gordon would come and go on his business trips, and things settled into a comfortable pattern.

It was a shock, therefore, to be woken in the early hours of a cold and rainy morning to the sound of the stable bell ringing loudly. The bell was connected to the main house and was rung whenever someone needed the stable yard.

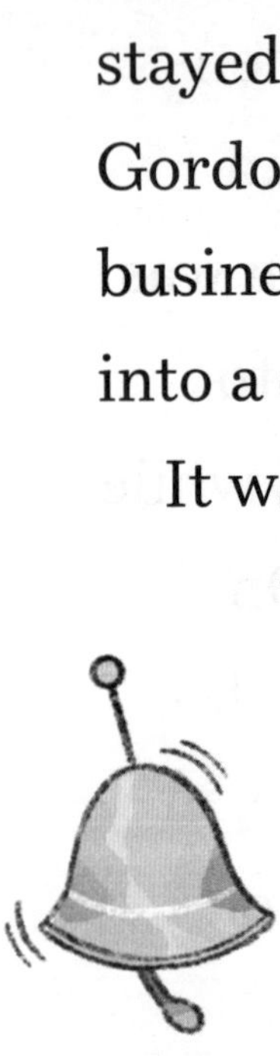

On this particular night, Joe had been left in charge until John returned in the morning. He woke with a fright at the clanging of the bell, then stumbled from his small room above the stables and into our stalls. It took him a moment to gather himself before he ran to the house. 'What is happening?' I asked.

Merrylegs shifted uneasily from leg to leg. 'I don't know, but if a horse is needed at this time of night, it can't be good news.'

Moments later, a flushed Joe came rushing back into the stables. 'Come on, Beauty,' he said breathlessly, taking me out of my stall and putting on my saddle. 'We're being sent for the doctor; the mistress is unwell.'

My heart thumped at Joe's words. Mrs Gordon had always been kind to me, and I believed I was a favourite of hers, too. To hear she was poorly worried me.

So, despite the wet, cold night, I galloped to the doctor's house a mile or so away. I was impressed at how well Joe rode me, but our journey back was harder as I also had the old doctor on my back.

Thoughts of Mrs Gordon pushed me on, straining my muscles and blinking away the rain. I did not want to waste precious time.

When we reached Birtwick, the doctor rushed into the house while I stood panting with the effort of the ride. I was looking forward to being safe and warm in my stall once again, but that was not to be.

Chapter Five

Although Joe had learnt a lot during his time at Birtwick, he was not yet a proper groom. A *proper* groom would have realised that a wet, cold horse needed to be rubbed dry, given fresh water and checked on after such a hard ride in the rain.

John would not be back until the morning and Joe was exhausted. After putting me back in my stall, he stumbled off to bed. 'What is he doing?' asked Ginger, whinnying and gently kicking her stall in frustration. 'You need to be rubbed down! You'll get ill!'

'It's all right, Ginger,' I said, although I could feel the cold seeping into my bones as I stood dripping on the floor of my stall.

'I'm sure Joe will sort me out in the morning.'

'It'll be too late by then!' Ginger said, getting more and more agitated.

'Calm yourself, Ginger!' said Merrylegs, firmly. 'You'll get into trouble! Beauty, try and rub yourself in the dry hay. You must keep as warm as you can.'

I took the old pony's advice, but nothing I did could keep me warm. I began to shiver, and as I slipped in and out of sleep, I could feel my head getting hotter and heavier. By the morning, I knew that I had caught a fever. I could not stand, and when John returned to the stable yard later that morning, I could see the panic in his face. 'Beauty!' he cried. 'What has happened to you? Joe! Get down here this instant!'

Joe, who had overslept after his night-time ride to fetch the doctor, rushed into the stall and turned pale when he saw me. He stutteringly explained what had happened and I could see John's face grow pink with anger. 'You left him soaking wet all night?' John bellowed. I had never heard

John's voice so loud. 'You stupid boy! You might have killed him! Fetch the veterinarian and be quick about it!'

Joe's eyes filled with tears as he ran out of the stables. John set to work, covering me with warm blankets and bringing oats mashed with warm milk for me to eat. All I wanted to do was sleep.

I did not know how long had passed before I opened my eyes to see the veterinarian, John and Squire Gordon kneeling in my stall. I tried to lift my head to show them I knew they were there. 'There, there, Beauty,' whispered John, soothingly. 'It's all going to be okay, boy.' Just beyond my stall I saw Joe, his face streaked with tears. Despite everything, I wanted him to know that I did not blame him.

That night I felt a little better and could breathe more easily.

John and Joe had not left my side.

'How is the patient?' asked Squire Gordon as he poked his head into my stall. He was in his evening clothes, and it looked as though the Gordons had guests for dinner.

I was touched that he had come to see me.

'Getting better, I am very glad to say,' said John, shooting a glare at Joe. 'I wasn't certain he would pull through. But it looks like he will.'

Squire Gordon sighed, happily.

'I am so glad,' he said. 'I have heard from the doctor that had Black Beauty not brought him to Mrs Gordon so quickly that night, she could have died. I owe this horse a lot.'

Hearing that Mrs Gordon would be okay was all I needed to raise my spirits and from that moment, I grew strong again.

Chapter Six

As soon as I was well again, Joe began working harder than ever. He started carrying a little notebook around with him in his back pocket and scribbled in it with an old pencil whenever John taught him something new. At night, he would sit on a haybale in our stables and read books about horses, waiting until he knew all

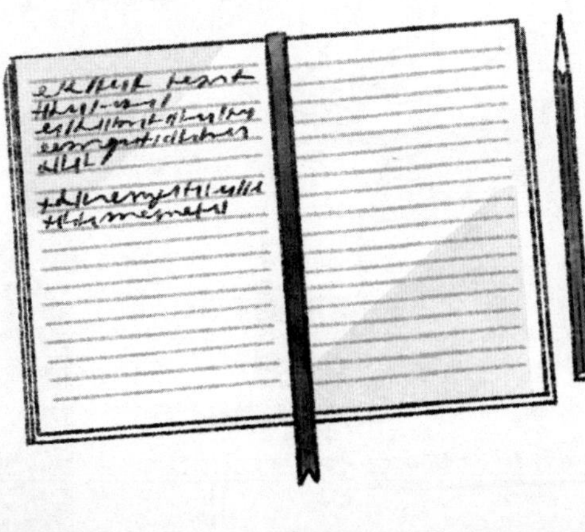

of us were settled and well before he went to bed himself. Soon, even John had to admit the young boy was growing into a good and attentive groom.

Although Mrs Gordon recovered from her illness, the doctor was still concerned about her health. She was prone to catching colds, and each one affected her worse than the one before. Eventually, the Gordons decided that they would move to a warmer country for a few years.

It was with a heavy heart that I parted from the Gordons. Merrylegs had been sold to the local vicar to pull his cart, and Joe went with him. Ginger and I were

prone

A habit, behaviour or event that is likely to happen often.

sold to friends of the Gordons, the Earl and Duchess of Westland. I was sad to say goodbye to old Merrylegs but overjoyed to still be with Ginger. Our new stables were just as comfortable as Birtwick, but the family were *very* different.

The duchess was a stern woman who seemed more concerned with how Ginger and I looked when we pulled her carriage, rather than

how comfortable we were. She made us wear bearing reins, a special type of rein that pulled our heads down to our chests to make us look "fashionable". I hated it, but I thought about my mother whenever I felt the urge to kick or struggle and tried to remain calm.

Ginger, however, did not take to wearing the reins so easily. She often thrashed her head from side to side, kicked her legs and gnashed her teeth. Her bad behaviour made the earl decide that she was not good enough to pull his carriage, and she was sent away to be trained as a hunting horse instead. From that day on I only saw Ginger now and then, galloping across the field, being ridden over and over again. I knew the work of a hunting horse would not suit her, and I wished I had managed to keep her calm.

As the months passed, I missed John and Joe and the Gordons. Although our new groom, York, was capable, he did not have their gentle touch. It was almost a relief, then, when I overheard York and the earl discussing a holiday the family were going to take. Aside from taking the family to the train station, I would not be needed, and York was told to take some time off too. A temporary groom was to be employed and I hoped he would be friendlier than York. I could not have imagined how wrong I was.

Chapter Seven

I was wary of Reuben Smith the moment he stepped into my stall. Although I had heard York say that he had many years of experience, it soon became clear that he was not a good groom. Smith did the least amount of work possible. He barely cleaned the stalls, and they soon became damp and smelly. He rode me without caution to the alehouse each night and rode back drunk and careless.

After a week, one of my hooves felt very sore. I had picked up a nail, but Smith did not notice nor care. When I slowed down or limped, he simply whipped me to go faster. I had never been so badly treated, and it was a shock. Eventually, my foot hurt me so much that on one of our trips back from the alehouse I fell to my knees in pain. Smith flew off my back and landed horribly on the ground, knocking himself out.

I struggled back to my feet, but my knees had been badly cut. There was nothing I could do.

It was dark, and I did not know the way back to the house. There was nothing I could do but wait there. After what seemed like hours, a small cart came down the lane. The horse saw me and whinnied. It was Ginger! The cart stopped and two of the earl's gardeners climbed out.

'It's old Smith! He's been thrown off!' cried one of the gardeners as he ran to see if Smith was okay. 'I didn't think Black Beauty was that kind of horse.'

'He's not,' the other gardener said grimly. 'Look at his hoof.

Smith has been riding him while he's lame. No wonder the poor horse fell.'

The two men picked up Smith and placed him in the back of the gardener's cart, then slowly and carefully led Ginger and me back

lame

When a person or animal is not able to walk well due to an injury or condition.

to the house. They patched me up as best they could, but they were not grooms and did not know the right way to deal with my cuts. My knees stung all night long, the blood seeping through my bandages. It was not until York returned from his time away that I was given proper treatment.

York cared for me in a more tender way than he ever had before. I think he felt guilty for leaving me with Smith, because he treated my knees and tried his best to make the scars look better. My legs had been left heavily marked, and it made me sad that my once sleek black legs now looked as they did.

When the earl and duchess returned home, the duchess took one look at my legs and declared that there was absolutely no way I could pull her carriage. She decided that I should be sold straight away, and so, without even being able to say goodbye to Ginger, I was loaded onto a cart and taken to the horse market.

Chapter Eight

Although I was not sad to be leaving the earl and duchess, I was frightened about what might happen to me next. The market was a noisy, dusty place. Horses of all shapes and sizes jostled for space in a large, fenced yard, while men with catalogues looked us over. A lot of people seemed to be interested in me, until they saw the scarring on

catalogue

An organised list of things such as book titles, goods for sale or other items.

my knees. 'This one's been badly treated,' said one man in a flat cap. 'He'll be a biter no doubt.'

I wished I could tell the men that I was a good horse. I tried to show them instead by standing still and tall and not getting spooked or frustrated by the prodding and poking hands.

Eventually, a small man with dark hair and kind eyes came over and stroked my nose. 'My, my, you are a fine fella,' he said, patting

my neck. He gently took my reins from York and walked me about the yard. The man instantly made me feel calm and I followed him obediently. 'I'll take him,' said the man when we returned to York. I was overjoyed.

My new owner was called Jerry. He strapped me to a cart alongside an older horse called Captain, and we began our journey. 'You been a taxi horse before, lad?' asked Captain, as we trotted side by side.

'A taxi horse?' I repeated, surprised. 'Are we not going to a farm or a house?'

Captain snorted a little laugh, but not in an unkind way. 'No, lad,' he said. 'We're off to London! Jerry is a taxi driver, and it's our job to drive his cab.'

The confusion must have shown on my face as Captain added: 'No need to worry, lad. I've had my share of masters and Mr Jerry is the best of 'em all. It's tiring work being a taxi horse, but that's why there's two of us – to share the load.'

I felt a little better at Captain's kind words, and was happier still when I met Jerry's family. London was busy, dirty and crowded, but the little street that housed Jerry, his wife, son and daughter was quieter than most. There was a small stable for me and Captain, a garage to hold the taxi and rooms above. Dolly, the youngest of Jerry's family, came out and softly stroked my nose. I nuzzled into her and she giggled with delight. Harry, who was about the same age as Joe when I had first met him, offered me a carrot and I munched on it gratefully.

Polly, Jerry's wife, was impressed with my looks – she did not even mention the scars on my legs. 'You'll be driving all sorts of fancy people with a horse like that!' she said, happily. 'Now, let me feed him before I feed the lot of you.'

That night, I fell asleep feeling more content and at peace than I had in a long time. Although the stables were not very fine, they were clean and dry, and Polly made the most delicious bran mash I had ever eaten. I was more than ready to start my new life with Jerry and Captain.

Chapter Nine

Life as a taxi horse was very different to anything I had known before. Captain and I would take it in turns to drive the taxi. As the youngest and fittest horse, I worked during the morning rush, taking gentlemen to the station and ladies to their appointments. Then, at lunchtime, Jerry would swap us over and Harry would give me a groom and a rest.

Most of the streets were stone or cobbled, and Jerry knew them all like the back of his hand. We went down narrow side lanes and up large tree-lined avenues,

through busy, bustling markets and even, once or twice, we passed an incredibly grand and large house that Jerry told me was Buckingham Palace where Queen Victoria lived.

One morning, we had just dropped off a fare when Jerry spotted a young woman on the side of the road. She was cradling a small child in a blanket and looked very frightened. 'Can I help you, Miss?' Jerry called from the top of the taxi.

'Could you tell me the way to St Thomas's hospital?' she asked. 'I need to take my little one there.'

'Hop in,' said Jerry, climbing down to open the door for the young woman. 'I'll take you myself.'

fare

The price paid to ride on a bus, train, taxi, or aeroplane; or a passenger who pays this price.

‘I’m sorry,’ she said, her cheeks flushing red. ‘I think there’s been a mistake. I don’t have any money for a taxi, I was just hoping you could point me in the right direction.’

Jerry smiled at the young woman. ‘Don’t worry about all that,’ he said kindly. ‘You’ve got a little one that needs caring for, that’s more important than money. Besides, it’s a fair-old walk to St Thomas’s. Make yourself comfy; we’ll be there in no time.’

My heart filled with pride at the kindness of my master. I knew how important it was to get medical help quickly. Once the woman and child were on the carriage, I trotted a little faster and with as much care as I could.

When we reached St Thomas's, Jerry helped the young woman to the door and, with tears in her eyes, she thanked him. An older, well-dressed lady stopped and stared at them both. 'Jerry?' she asked. 'It *is* you, isn't it? You drove my sister and I to lots of parties last winter! What are you doing here?'

'He's being kind,' said the young mother, who proceeded to tell the older woman what Jerry had done for her, before rushing her child inside the hospital.

The well-dressed woman looked very impressed, and asked Jerry to take her to the station. She had been visiting a friend in the hospital and was now on her way home. She offered to pay for the young mother's fare, as well as her own, but Jerry would not take the extra money. 'Very well,' replied the woman. 'In that case, take my contact card instead. If you ever grow tired of being a taxi driver, my household can always use a groom who knows horses as well as you do – and who is as kind as you are.'

Jerry slipped the card into his pocket, and we carried on with our morning.

Chapter Ten

My time passed happily in London. Although the work was hard, I was strong and in my prime. I learnt how to dodge the traffic and pick up my pace when needed. Jerry, however, was growing older. Harry occasionally joined us on our morning shifts, but he was not quite old enough to take on the taxi himself.

prime

The time when a person, animal or object is at its best.

One bitterly cold winter, Jerry developed a bad cough. The cold air, and being out in all weathers, did not help and I could feel his grasp on my reins getting weaker and weaker.

'There now, boy,' Jerry said one particularly cold evening. He had come to place extra blankets over Captain and me. 'You've been one of the best horses I've ever owned, but it's time for a change.' He

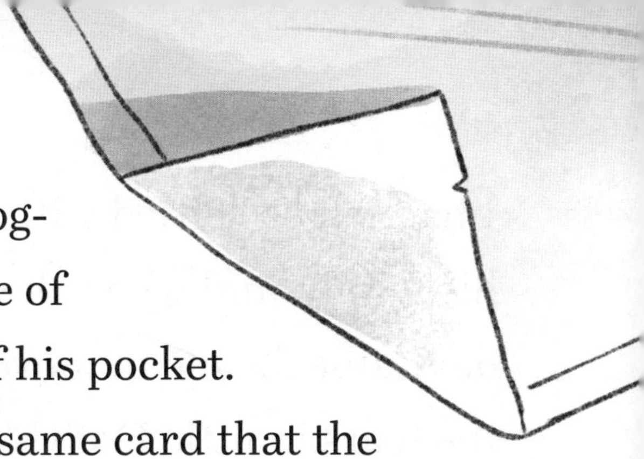

pulled a dog-eared piece of card out of his pocket. It was the same card that the elegant older lady had passed him a few years earlier. 'Remember this lady? She's offered me a job with a house out in the country. I wish I could take you with me, truth be told, but I can only take one of you. Captain is old. No one will have him if I leave him here, but you'll be all right. Strong horse like you. You'll be snapped up in no time.'

My heart thudded in my chest.

I had felt so settled with Jerry and his family, and when the dreaded day came for me to move on, I saw the tears in little Dolly's eyes. I had been sold to another taxi driver, or so I thought, called Skinner, who had wanted to buy me from Jerry for a long time.

Skinner led me to a warehouse in a strange and unfamiliar part of London. There were other horses lined up and tied together and to my joy, I spotted Ginger!

'I am so glad to see you again!' I said, when Skinner tied me up next to the other horses. Ginger looked tired and thin. Her once beautiful mane was matted and her back looked sore.

'Oh Beauty,' she said. 'What a time I have had since I last saw you. I have been sold over and over again until last year I ended up in this *place*.'

Ginger explained that different people came to the warehouse to hire horses for a day, a week or a month at a time. The horses were hired for all sorts of reasons, and no one really seemed to care what those reasons were. Sometimes the people who hired the horses were good riders, but most of the time they treated them badly. It was not much better when the horses were left in the warehouse.

'Where are the stables?' I asked, looking around.

'These *are* the stables,' Ginger replied.

I looked at the dirty hard floor with its wisps of hay, the muddy-looking water in the trough and shuddered at the thought of what life was going to be like from now on.

Chapter Eleven

We were known as cab horses. To be hired and left at random. One day I might be pulling a carriage into the countryside, the next a great cart filled with heavy barrels around London. I was driven by

people who did not know what they were doing or did not care. I was never groomed, and the place where Ginger and I slept, with the rest of the cab horses, was dirty and never cleaned out.

Ginger had been a cab horse for longer than I had and soon she was being hired out less and less. The customers saw how weak she had become and did not pick her.

One day, she was led out of the warehouse, and I never saw her again.

After Ginger left the warehouse, I lost a bit of hope. My life seemed like an endless cycle of mistreatment and hard work. The diamond on my nose faded when I was covered in soot from a job in a coal yard and never got clean.

I longed for a warm stable, a groom to wash and care for me, a full trough of water and a big bowl of bran mash. At night I dreamt about my mother and when I woke, I was sad to realise I was not in the meadow at Farmer Grey's, but in the filthy warehouse about to start another day of work.

One morning, I was hired by a taxi driver, and although I knew the work, the driver was not as kind as Jerry. I hardly had any breaks and worked all day. In the evening, we picked a family up from outside a theatre. ‘Mummy, that poor horse doesn’t look very well,’ cried the little girl.

'He's all right, miss!' said the taxi driver cheerfully. 'Now hop on board and we'll get you home.'

The family lived at the top of a very steep hill, lined with tall townhouses. A fine rain began to fall, making the road slick beneath my feet and slowing my pace.

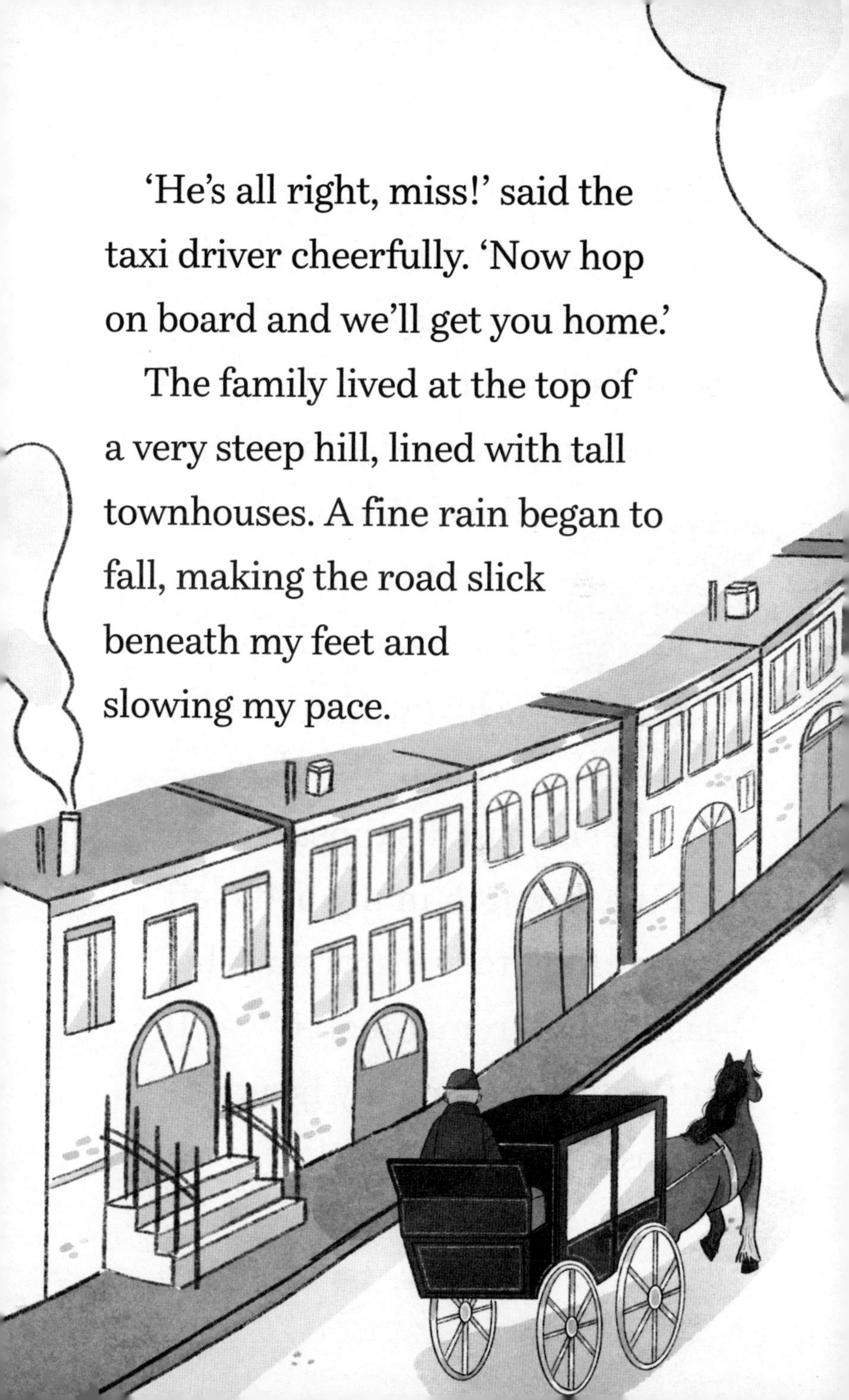

The taxi driver whipped me across my shoulders, and I winced at the pain. 'Hurry up you old nag!' he hissed.

I blinked away the rain. Up ahead, I saw a beautiful horse that looked just like Duchess, my mother. When I blinked again, she had disappeared and all the strength in my body left me as I fell to the ground. The last thing I remembered was the little girl stroking my head as I closed my eyes.

I woke up in the warehouse again. Skinner was ranting and raving at one of the men at the warehouse. 'I had to give the man a full refund!' he shouted. 'And get another horse and cart out to go and fetch the old brute! What good is he to me now?'

'Sell 'im then,' said the other man. 'Feed 'im up a bit and sell 'im on before anyone realises he's no good.'

Skinner scratched his chin and glared at me. I stared back, hard, even though it was something my mother had told me never to do to a master. I wanted to show Skinner that he had not broken my spirit.

Chapter Twelve

For the next two weeks I was not hired out on any jobs. I stayed in the warehouse and was fed well. I began to regain the weight I had lost and the bones that had started to show on my hips and ribs did not look so bad. As soon as he was able, Skinner took me to a horse market.

Once again, men came and prodded and poked me, feeling my legs and looking at my teeth.

They tutted and shook their heads. The sale went on and the crowd of customers thinned until only a few remained.

'Grandpa, Grandpa, look at this one!' cried a young boy.

'He's a bit old, Willie,' said an older man with a thin white beard and tweed coat.

'No, he's not, he just needs a clean. Take a look, Grandpa, please!' Willie insisted.

Willie's grandfather was a farmer called Mr Thoroughgood. He began his inspection, gently looking at my teeth, my eyes, the scars on my knees and the state of my hooves. 'I think you might be right, Willie,' he said, eventually. 'How much is he?'

'Can't take less than twenty pounds for him,' Skinner said.

Mr Thoroughgood stared at Skinner, then back at me. 'I'll give you fourteen pounds, and I won't report you for the mistreatment of this animal. It's clear you've worked him to the bone and not looked after him.'

Skinner's eyes widened and he quickly accepted the money Mr Thoroughgood handed to him. 'Now, see you don't let any of your other horses get in this state. I'll be keeping my eye on you!' Mr Thoroughgood said, taking my reins and leading me out of the horse market.

Mr Thoroughgood's farm reminded me of Farmer Grey's. Tears welled in my eyes when

I stepped into my meadow. Willie and Mr Thoroughgood gave me a good bath and I watched the grime and muck wash away with delight. They uncovered the diamond on my nose and my single white foot and thought I was a very handsome

horse, despite my scarred legs and thin body.

I was fitted with new shoes, which felt wonderful, and given as many bowls of bran mash as I could eat. My stables were warm and dry, and at long last I slept well again.

After a month of care from Mr Thoroughgood and Willie, I felt like my old self. I had filled out and my coat and mane were shiny. My tail swished happily as I trotted around the meadow with Willie on my back.

'My, my, he's like a different

horse!' said Mr Thoroughgood, climbing over a fence and into the meadow. 'I think he might be ready for his new home.'

Chapter Thirteen

The thought of leaving Mr Thoroughgood and Willie filled me with fear. I thought I had found a home at last and had not realised that I was going to be sold again. The following day, Mr Thoroughgood strapped me to his cart, and we drove a short way out into a village.

We pulled up outside a sweet-looking cottage and Mr Thoroughgood jumped down to knock on the door. Two older, well-dressed women appeared.

'He's beautiful!' said one of the women. 'What is his name?'

'We don't know, Miss Ellen,'

replied Mr Thoroughgood. 'He came to us in a bad way, but young

Willie has an eye for the good horses, and we soon cleaned him up.'

'He looks like he falls a lot,' said the other woman. 'Look at the scars on his legs.'

'He's a fine rider, Miss Blomefield,' said Mr Thoroughgood. 'But a bad owner can make any horse fall.'

Miss Blomefield moved closer, and I stood proud and tall to show her I was a well-behaved horse.

‘Well, Miss Ellen and Miss Blomefield,’ said Mr Thoroughgood, nodding at the two women in turn. ‘I will wait to hear your decision.’

As we drove back to the farm, I thought about the two women. If they were to be my new masters, I would be very happy.

A few days later, I was in the meadow enjoying a soft breeze on my face when I saw Mr Thoroughgood and another man striding towards me through the grass. The man was tall and broad, with bright red hair and a red beard. ‘Here he is,’ said Mr

Thoroughgood, giving me a strong pat on my back. 'If it were up to my Willie, he would be staying with us forever, but I think he's just the right horse for your mistresses.'

'Miss Ellen liked him right enough,' said the man. 'Miss

Blomefield will take some convincing. That's why she sent me to have another look at him. They want me to be their groom, you see.' The man began the usual checks, looking at my teeth and hooves. He was gentle, but I instantly got the feeling he knew what he was doing. His touch reminded me of John, all those years ago at the Gordons'.

When he finished, the man stepped back and looked me over. A strange expression came over his face. 'What's the matter, Joe?' asked Mr Thoroughgood.

'You look like you have seen a ghost!'

'Beauty?' gasped the man. 'Black Beauty, is that you?'

Chapter Fourteen

No one had called me Black Beauty since I had left Jerry and his family. My ears pricked up instantly and I stared at the man.

It was Joe! Young Joe from Birtwick, who had made a bad mistake but learnt from it. And now here he was all grown up. Oh, how I wished I could ask him a thousand questions.

'Do you know this horse?' asked Mr Thoroughgood, looking amazed.

'I do,' said Joe. 'I'd know that diamond nose and white hoof anywhere. No other horse I have ever worked with has that same proud look about him.'

Joe stepped closer and stroked

my nose and I nuzzled into his hand to show him that I recognised him, too. 'Have you forgiven me, old boy?' he asked. 'When I was starting out as a groom, this horse taught me a valuable lesson. I have often wondered what happened to him.'

Soon afterwards, Miss Ellen and Miss Blomefield bought me to pull their small carriage, and for their servant to ride on for errands. The stables were small and cosy, with an apartment above for Joe.

Miss Ellen was a confident rider, but it took Miss Blomefield a long time to trust me. It was a few months before she drove the carriage on her own. I took the roads carefully and more slowly than I would have liked, to make sure she knew she could rely on me.

One day, I heard Joe telling his mistresses what he knew of my story. He had no idea what had happened to me after he left with Merrylegs, or how I had gotten my scars. Joe explained that when the Gordons came back to England, they had tried to find out what had happened to Ginger and me.

They were angry that the earl and duchess had sold both of us without letting them know. Miss Ellen clapped her hands together. 'I shall write to Mrs Gordon!' she said. 'I am sure she will want to know that one of her old horses is safe and well with us.'

Miss Ellen was correct, and a few days after sending her letter she received a reply from Mrs

Gordon, asking if she could come and see me as soon as it was convenient. She also added that if they ever needed to sell me for any reason, they should contact her immediately. I would always be welcome there. It warmed my heart to hear it.

Life was quiet and comfortable with Miss Ellen, Miss Blomefield and Joe. I had finally found a home I could call my own. I knew I would be safe here, and well looked after for the rest of my days.

As I settled into my warm stable one night, a trough full of feed and clean, comfy hay all around me, I thought about all the horses I had known in my life.

I was grateful that I had got to see Ginger again, despite the terrible conditions we both had to work in. I would never forget the happier times we had together. I also thought fondly of Merrylegs, old Captain and, of course, Duchess, my mother.

Her advice had kept me safe more times than I could possibly count over the years. She was strong and good, and I hoped more than anything that she would be proud of me and the life I had led.

Above all, I felt so very lucky to

have ended up here and from that day on, I woke up each morning feeling as happy as it was possible for a horse to feel and determined to keep making my mother proud.

Anna Sewell

Anna Sewell was born in Norfolk in 1820. Her concern for horses began at an early age. Horsepower was an important means of transportation in the 1800s, but Sewell wanted people to be compassionate about the animals. After falling ill with a disease that meant Sewell could no longer leave her house, she devoted seven years to writing *Black Beauty* – the only book she ever published. Although intended for adults, *Black Beauty* is famous as a children's novel.